Captain Blownaparte™
and the Golden Skeleton

by Helga Hopkins & David Benham

Part Two: The Golden Arm

Part 2 - The Golden Arm

Captain Blownaparte and his crew were tucking into a very large fish pie. The Golden Skull watched them enviously, because fish pie had been his favourite dish in the days before a nasty ghost captain turned him into a golden skeleton. Now all his golden bones are hidden in different and dangerous places, but Captain Blownaparte and his crew are helping him to find them so he can become human again. Happily, Captain Blownaparte has already found the golden neck bones. 'Next we're going to look for one of the golden arms,' chuckled Captain Blownaparte. 'Yes indeed, but I wish it wasn't hidden in the cave of a frightening sea serpent!' grumbled Alfredo. But fortified by the delicious fish pie, they all sailed on towards the sea serpent's cave.

Soon they arrived at the cave, but the serpent had spotted the ship and suddenly shot out of the water and grabbed Captain Blownaparte by his shiny hook-hand. 'Oh pleeeease don't eat him!' screamed little Sproggie. 'All those metal bits attached to the Captain will give you the most terrible tummy ache!' Then as the crew watched in horror, the serpent dropped the Captain and angrily grabbed Sproggie instead!

Luckily, the serpent quickly had a change of heart and dropped Sproggie back on the ship's deck. 'I'm not hungry anyway, but I'll behave myself if you help me find my missing wife - Mrs Sea Serpent. Some nasty pirates recently captured her and took her away to sell to a circus! She's being kept on a secret island and I've been searching for her ever since.' Captain Blownaparte nodded knowingly. 'OK, If you give us the golden arm, we'll help you find your wife.' 'And I can tell you something about this nasty business too,' said Alfredo' 'I heard that Captain Specklebeard is the pirate who has a sea serpent locked away somewhere, and that he keeps a map of the secret island in his back pocket.'

Captain Specklebeard was the owner of a very dodgy pirate tavern. So with Sproggie in tow, Captain Blownaparte set off to retrieve the map. Prosper the clever parrot, and Turnip the pet rat, hurried along behind them as usual, determined to join the fun. When they arrived at the tavern, they quietly peered through one of the dusty windows. The tavern was full of extremely fierce looking pirates. 'Oh my goodness!' grumbled Sproggie, 'Specklebeard is wearing a kilt, so his trousers with the map in the pocket must be upstairs. What on earth shall we do now?'

'Leave this to me,' said Turnip, letting out an ear splitting whistle! Seconds later they were surrounded by a band of rats in all shapes and sizes. 'These are my dear cousins,' said Turnip proudly! 'And how exactly is this going to help us?' enquired Prosper. 'Well you see, with the exception of Captain Blownaparte, all pirates are traditionally afraid of rats', said Turnip. 'Just watch this!' Turnip whistled again, and all his cousins streamed into the tavern. Inside, there was a sudden deathly silence. Frozen to the spot, the pirates stared at the rats in total shock. Then, pushing and shoving each other they clambered up on the wobbly tables and chairs in a blind panic. There they all stood up on tippy-toes, holding on to each other for safety. 'You see!' said Turnip proudly. 'Problem solved!'

Sproggie and Captain Blownaparte rushed past the cowering pirates and ran upstairs to Captain Specklebeard's bedroom. When they opened the door they couldn't believe their eyes. Specklebeard's clothes were moving around the room! The nightshirt was dancing with the trousers and the socks were twirling around on the ceiling. 'Pooooooh!!' said Prosper. 'These clothes have never EVER been washed! They're so smelly, they've taken on a life of their own. When we get the map we'll have to run fast, or the clothes will come running after us!' With everyone tightly holding their noses, Prosper swiftly plucked the map from the back pocket of Specklebeard's trousers, and flew off out of the window gasping for air! The Captain, Sproggie and Turnip made their getaway down the stairs, but sure enough the smelly clothes were flapping along right behind them!

When they reached the water's edge, the Captain pushed the rowing boat into the water and started rowing like mad. Sproggie shrieked as a dirty nightshirt grabbed him round the neck and tried to pull him out of the boat, but Captain Blownaparte sliced his cutlass leg right through the nightshirt's grubby sleeves and rowed away even faster! 'That was a close shave!' panted Sproggie, looking back at the stinky socks and smelly pyjamas which were angrily jumping up and down on the beach!

Opening the map, they saw where the secret island was – it was Palm Island, about two hours away, and Captain Specklebeard had drawn a big red cross on the map showing where Mrs Sea Serpent was being held. They set sail straight away, and after about an hour, they suddenly saw the Sea Serpent's head bobbing up from under the water right alongside them. 'Is this as fast as you can go?' he grumbled. 'D'you mind if I speed the ship up a bit?' And with a slithery twirl, he wrapped his tail around the ship's figurehead and swam off at breakneck speed. Captain Blownaparte and the crew all tumbled backwards across the deck in utter amazement, they'd never travelled this fast before! Sproggie doubled up with laughter. 'I wish we always had an outboard serpent to pull us along like this!'

With the serpent's help they quickly reached the secret island, where their new found friend offered to keep watch over the ship during the search for Mrs Serpent. Before long, Captain Blownaparte realised the island was made up entirely of big boulders which was going to make the search extremely difficult. Everyone was becoming very tired but still continued searching. 'Hey! There's an opening in the rocks!' Turnip suddenly screamed. He squeezed into a secret shaft going down between the rocks, but promptly started to slide down rather quickly! Sproggie tried to grab him but lost his footing and started to slide down too. Desperately, Rosie grabbed Sproggie's leg, but she couldn't stop him and tumbled down the shaft as well! Captain Blownaparte stood peering down the narrow hole in horror. 'What on earth will become of them now?' he asked Alfredo.

Meanwhile Turnip and his friends slid down the shaft which opened into a huge cave containing a very deep lake. One after the other they plopped into the lake, but were able to swim to the rocky edges and clamber out. As they all sat there shivering and blowing their noses, Sproggie reminded everyone to keep an eye out for Mrs Serpent.

It didn't take long before the giant head of Mrs Serpent appeared out of the lake. She looked them over, and grumpily sniffed them up and down. 'The food portions in here are getting smaller and smaller!' Then taking a closer look at tiny Turnip, she complained that this little furry one wasn't even enough to fill a tooth! But when Turnip heard this he really lost his temper and paddled towards the serpent and screamed at her, 'I'm not a tasty meal, you silly serpent, I'm here to save you!'

Mrs Serpent wasn't listening and was just about to swallow Turnip when Prosper swooped in as fast as lightning. Just in time he grabbed Turnip and whisked him out of harm's way. Then he flew up onto the serpent's head and explained that they were all only there to save her, and that her husband was waiting for her down at the water's edge. 'We'll be lucky if we ever get out of here,' sighed the serpent. 'The door is always locked and the key is hung on a nail on the other side of the door.' They all looked desperately at the huge heavy door. 'All is not lost,' said Prosper, who'd had a clever idea. 'Turnip can crawl under that gap at the bottom of the door, get the key, and push it back to us under the gap.'

Turnip was not so keen, the gap looked really small – even for him! Rosie and Sproggie tried hard to push him through the gap, but every time they pushed, Turnip squealed loudly. Mrs Serpent began to get impatient, and pushed Sproggie and Rosie out of the way. Then with one almighty shove, she forced Turnip through the gap. 'Are you OK?' asked Sproggie looking a bit concerned. 'What do you think? complained Turnip. 'I'll need at least an hour to count my legs and whiskers!' 'Yes, but before you do that, could you please let us have the key!' pleaded Rosie. They heard a rustling followed by a clanking as the giant key was squeezed under the door. They were free!

Back at the entrance to the shaft, Captain Blownaparte was becoming desperately worried. 'What if Mrs Serpent has eaten Rosie and Sproggie?' 'And Turnip too!' blabbered Alfredo, wiping the tears from his eyes. 'What DO you mean?' said a sudden voice from behind them. 'I DON'T eat my friends!' Looking back over their shoulders, the crew were mightily relieved to see the lost group up on Mrs Serpent's slippery back and hanging on for dear life! Everyone was overcome with happiness, and Alfredo's tears changed into the biggest smile you've ever seen!

They all hurried back to the ship where the two serpents embraced and thanked the Captain and his crew for bringing them back together again. Then, with a happy hoot, they curled both their tails around the ship's figurehead and doubled the speed back home to the harbour where Mr Sea Serpent handed over the golden arm as promised.

As the sun went down, Captain Blownaparte and his crew licked their lips as they waited to begin the ship's customary feast, which they all looked forward to after every exciting adventure. Sproggie began reaching for a tasty looking pie, but the Captain stopped him in his tracks and announced, 'No one eats before the Golden Skull is reunited with his arm!' Alfredo agreed, but also began to grumble about the dangers of finding where the other golden bones were hidden. 'We'll think about that after the grand feast!' beamed Captain Blownaparte, rubbing his hungry tummy which was beginning to make funny gurgling noises. Finally, as Sproggie was given the honour of attaching the arm onto the delighted Golden Skull, they all began a very noisy evening.

The End

PEDRO

ROSIE

PROSPER

CAPTAIN
BLOWNAPARTE

SPROGGIE

SPIKE

TURNIP

PIRATE TIDY

ALFREDO

SWISS SEPP

Printed in Great Britain
by Amazon

24606646R00023